CU00871936

508

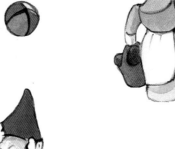

First published in Great Britain by HarperCollins Publishers Ltd in 1997

1 3 5 7 9 10 8 6 4 2

Copyright © 1997 Enid Blyton Company Ltd. Enid Blyton's signature mark and the word
'NODDY' are Registered Trade Marks of Enid Blyton Ltd.

ISBN 0 00 136092 2

Cover design and illustrations by County Studios
A CIP catalogue for this title is available from the British Library.
All rights reserved. No part of this publication may be reproduced, stored in a retrieval
system or transmitted in any form or by any means, electronic, mechanical, photocopying,
recording or otherwise, without the prior permission of HarperCollins Publishers Ltd,
77-85 Fulham Palace Road, Hammersmith, London W6 8JB.

Printed and bound in Belgium by Proost

NODDY™

TOYLAND STORIES

Enid Blyton™

Collins

An Imprint of HarperCollinsPublishers

THIS BOOK BELONGS TO

CONTENTS

A Letter from Noddy

Hallo, girls and boys!

I'm your friend Noddy! When I nod my head, the bell on my hat goes 'jingle-jingle', and everyone knows it's me.

I live in a little house called "House-for-One" which I built myself! It's got a garage for my little yellow car, which I use for driving my Toyland friends wherever they want to go. They have to pay me sixpence, though!

I've got lots of friends in Toyland – the Tubby Bears, Bumpy-Dog, Mr Plod the policeman and many more. My very best friend is dear old Big-Ears. He lives in a Toadstool House in the woods. In this book you can read about some of our adventures. I'm sure you will enjoy them as much as we did!

I've promised to take Mrs Tubby Bear to the shops, so goodbye for now!

Love from

Noddy

Big-Ears and the
Naughty Trick

Big-Ears was busy washing his bicycle. He had a big sponge and a bowl of soapy water. His bicycle was going to be sparkling when he had finished!

"Mmm, it's certainly very clean," Big-Ears said to himself thoughtfully when at last all the washing was done. "But it's not very shiny. I'll pop into my house and see if I have any bicycle polish left."

The moment Big-Ears had gone, two figures appeared from behind the trees. It was the goblins! They crept towards Big-Ears' bicycle to play a mean trick on him. Big-Ears was in his house for quite a while.

He searched every cupboard for some bicycle polish. But there was not a trace to be found! "Oh, why didn't I remember to buy some polish when I went to Toy Town this morning?" Big-Ears tutted crossly as he stepped out of his house again. "I can be so forgetful sometimes. I'll just have to ride all the way to Toy Town again!"

But just as Big-Ears was about to climb onto his bicycle, he spotted a large round tin in the basket. It was a tin of bicycle polish! "Now where did that suddenly come from?" he asked himself, mystified. He stroked his beard. "It must have been there all the time," he said, starting to CHUCKLE. "I must have bought some polish this morning, after all!" Big-Ears chuckled again and again, as he started to polish his bicycle.

"I must be getting even more forgetful than I thought!" he grinned. Big-Ears polished and polished until his bicycle gleamed like a new pin.

"Perfect!" he smiled. "I've never seen my bicycle looking so shiny. I'm so proud of it, I think I'll just go for a little ride before putting it away!"

So Big-Ears climbed on to his bicycle.

"Just a very short ride," he promised himself. "And a very careful one, too. I don't want to ride my bicycle into any puddles or I'll have to wash and polish it all over again!"

As soon as Big-Ears started to pedal, though, he rode right into a puddle.

He had wanted to go *forwards* but his bicycle had gone *backwards* instead.

"That's strange," Big-Ears said to himself. "I'm sure I was pedalling the right way. Now, let me try again."

This time Big-Ears was even *more* careful, but again exactly the same thing happened. His bicycle went *backwards!* "Perhaps I'm on a bit of a slope and my bicycle keeps running downhill," Big-Ears said with a frown. "I'll try pedalling much faster this time."

SPLASH! SQUELCH

Big-Ears pedalled as hard as he possibly could, and suddenly his bicycle went WHOOSH!

"Oh dear! Oh deary me!" Big-Ears cried, as his bicycle sped backwards, weaving between the trees. "Help, someone! HELP!"

Suddenly Big-Ears turned his head and saw a large dip in the ground.

"Oh no!" he cried.

BUMP! BUMPITY BUMP!

"Goodness, now I'm sore!"

But something even more dangerous was approaching from behind. It was Noddy's car!

"Move to one side, Big-Ears!" Noddy shouted. "You're in the middle of the road. And why are you going *backwards*?"

Big-Ears clapped his hands over his ears as he heard a frantic

PARP! PARP! PARP! from Noddy's car. But there was nothing he could do. His bicycle would not stop speeding backwards.

"Look out!" Noddy cried. "You're going to hit my car!"

Fortunately, Noddy managed to steer his car out of the way just in time.

Big-Ears' problems were far from over, however. His bicycle kept going, bumping over the ground, until finally it rolled down the river bank.

"What's wrong with your bicycle all of a sudden?" Noddy asked, as he helped pull Big-Ears out of the river. "It seems to have gone mad!"

"Yes, it does, doesn't it?" Big-Ears said very crossly. "And I think I've just worked out why. You see, I found a tin of polish in my basket. But it was no ordinary polish. It made my bicycle go the wrong way!"

"Well, who could have put it in your basket?" asked Noddy.

"It must have been the goblins," said Big-Ears.

"Oh, of course!" exclaimed Noddy. "Who else would play such a naughty trick?"

Big-Ears suddenly shivered. He was longing to get back to his Toadstool House so he could dry himself by a nice cosy fire. But first he had a job to do.

"Can I give you a lift home, Big-Ears?" asked Noddy.

"No, thank you, Noddy," he said, climbing onto his bicycle. "I have worked out that if I pedal backwards, I will go forwards."

But when Big-Ears started to pedal backwards, the bicycle also went backwards. Again, he ended up in the river!

"The water must have washed the goblins' polish off," Noddy said, as he helped pull Big-Ears out of the river again. "Try pedalling forwards this time."

This is exactly what Big-Ears did and, sure enough, the bicycle went forwards. "Hurrah!" cheered Noddy. "Will you be going straight back home now?"

"Not quite yet," replied Big-Ears. "First, I'm going to pay the goblins a visit. And to get my own back on them, I'm going to pretend that my bicycle is still out of control. So they had better WATCH THEIR TOES!" he said, with a hearty chuckle.

MR SPARKS

TO THE RESCUE

It was a very exciting day for Mr Sparks. He had a new car-wash at the garage.

"I'll just check that everything works," he said to himself proudly. He turned on the tap. He could hear a nice **gurgle, gurgle** inside the hose. Then he went to the other end of the hose. "That's funny," he said, as he lifted the hose. "Where is the water?"

But at that very moment the water started to gush out, *SQUIRTING* him in the face.

"Ah, it works perfectly!" Mr Sparks said with delight. "All I need now are some customers!"

It was not very long before Mr Sparks heard a PARP, PARP coming in his direction.

"Ah," he said to himself with a smile. "That must be Noddy's car!"

Mr Sparks was hoping that Noddy's car would not be very clean. He was in luck. As the little car came into view, Mr Sparks saw that it was not quite as shiny as usual.

"Hello, Noddy!" Mr Sparks called. "Would you like to try my brand new car-washing service? It will make your car nice and clean again."

"Will it?" Noddy asked eagerly. "I've been so busy giving people rides this morning that I haven't had time to clean it myself."

"It will only take five minutes,"

Mr Sparks said. "Just jump out of your car and I'll switch on my special hose."

So Noddy switched off his engine while Mr Sparks went into the garage to turn on the tap. But just then, it started to rain *very* heavily!

"I won't be needing your car-wash after all, Mr Sparks," Noddy called. "My car will get clean in the rain!" And at that, Noddy turned on his engine.

"But, Noddy!" Mr Sparks called after him as he came out of the garage. "NODDY!"

He was too late, though. Noddy and his car were gone.

"Well, I can't blame him," Mr Sparks muttered to himself. "Who wants a car-wash in the rain? I'll just have to hope that the rain soon stops."

But the rain did not stop. It just became heavier and heavier.

Poor Mr Sparks. His new car-wash was not going to be busy today!

"Perhaps I'll have more luck with my breakdown truck," Mr Sparks said to himself. "I'll drive it around Toy Town and see if anyone needs help."

But Mr Sparks was not lucky with his breakdown truck either.

He drove it all the way to the harbour and all the way back again but he did not meet one car. Where was everyone?

"I suppose no one wants to go out in heavy rain like this," he grumbled. "What a miserable day I'm having!"

Mr Sparks was not the only one who was having a miserable day. Noddy was, too. He suddenly appeared at Mr Sparks' garage. And he was *very* wet and *very* cross.

"Mr Sparks, you must help me," he said. "After I left you, I drove to Big-Ears' house to see if I could borrow an umbrella."

"Very wise with all the rain, Noddy," Mr Sparks said. Then he lifted his hat to scratch his head. "But where is the umbrella, Noddy? You're as wet as a fish!"

"I never reached Big-Ears' house," Noddy explained. "The rain had made it so muddy in the Dark Wood that my car got stuck. I need your breakdown truck to pull it out!"

Mr Sparks was delighted to be able to help. "Just wait here, Noddy. I'll fetch the truck."

Soon they were ready to set off. "Don't worry, Noddy, we'll be at the Dark Wood in a flash!" said Mr Sparks.

And in a flash they were. Noddy's car looked such a sorry sight stuck in the mud. The mud came halfway up the tyres!

"Never mind, Noddy," said Mr Sparks. "My truck will soon pull your car out." Mr Sparks pressed a special button in his truck so that the big hook at the back started to come down.

When it was low enough, Mr Sparks attached it to Noddy's car. Mr Sparks then sat in his truck and started the engine. He made the engine go a bit faster, then a bit faster. At first nothing happened. But then it started to move forward very slowly. And Noddy's car started to move as well!

"Oh, thank you, Mr Sparks, thank you!" Noddy cried. "My car isn't stuck any more!"

Mr Sparks was also delighted. He loved using his breakdown truck. And this was not the only business he would be doing today. Noddy's car now needed a very good clean and this time there was no rain to do the job.

"It looks as if you'll have to use my new car-wash after all, Noddy!" Mr Sparks chuckled.

Mr Plod and
the Stolen Bicycle

It was a very dull day in Toyland.

"I do wish something exciting would happen," grumbled Mr Plod.

Around the corner rushed Big-Ears, puffing and panting. He bumped right into the policeman.

"Assaulting an officer of the law, are we?" asked Mr Plod crossly.

"You must help me!" Big-Ears gasped. "My bicycle was stolen as I was picking mushrooms in the woods."

"That is a serious crime indeed," said Mr Plod. "I must investigate at once!"

The policeman went to the place where mushrooms grew. It was the darkest, most frightening part of the woods. As he walked through the trees, the leaves beneath his feet CRUNCHED and the twigs CRACKLED.

"It is an offence for an officer of the law to be frightened," Mr Plod told himself sternly. He whistled loudly to make himself feel brave. Suddenly the policeman heard a rustling sound. Nervously he shone his torch high into the trees. Two blackbirds were building their nest. He crouched down and peered beneath some bushes. A family of rabbits scampered out of sight.

"AHH!" Mr Plod nearly jumped out of his skin as a squirrel ran over his foot. "I should arrest you for frightening a police officer!" he shouted angrily.

Then Mr Plod tripped and fell to the ground.

THUD!

"What on earth...?" he cried, getting up.

He had fallen over a mushroom basket. Big-Ears must have dropped it when the thief stole his bicycle!

"A clue!" said Mr Plod excitedly. But where was Big-Ears' bicycle now?

The policeman bent down. There on the ground was a tyre track which led deeper into the woods.

"Aha! The thief must have taken Big-Ears' bicycle this way," said Mr Plod, and he crept quietly along, following the track.

A stream trickled through the woods. But Mr Plod was following the track so carefully that he didn't notice the stream at all.

Until...

He was up to his knees in water! "Oh, bother!" he exclaimed. By now Mr Plod was very wet, very cold and very cross.

He climbed soggily out of the stream and saw in front of him a shabby little hut. The tyre track led right to its door!

Wanting to be as quiet as possible, Mr Plod got down on all fours and crawled slowly towards the hut. When he reached it, he peeped nervously in through the open door. Something hit him right in the face!

"STOP, IN THE NAME OF THE LAW!" Mr Plod shouted. But it was only a pigeon flying out of the hut.

Mr Plod looked round, and there in the corner was Big-Ears' bicycle. There was no sign of the thief.

"I've had quite enough excitement for one day!" Mr Plod sighed, climbing onto the bicycle. "And at least I *have* recovered stolen property!" He began to cycle slowly back towards Toy Town.

Mr Plod was almost home when he heard a familiar PARP! PARP!

"That's young Noddy's car," he said. Sure enough, as he cycled around the corner, he saw Noddy's car in the middle of the road.

"Causing an obstruction, are we?" Mr Plod asked sternly.

"Oh, Mr Plod, thank goodness you're here," Noddy cried. "My little car has stopped and I need someone strong like you to give me a push."

"Jump in and I'll soon have you moving again," said Mr Plod, climbing from the bicycle.

He leaned forward and pushed the car with all his might. It did not move. He turned round and pushed it with his bottom. It still did not move. He sat down on the bumper wondering what to do next. The car zoomed away and Mr Plod fell to the ground.

"That's all the thanks I get!" grumbled the policeman. He picked himself up and climbed wearily back onto Big-Ears' bicycle.

As he approached Toy Town, Mr Plod could hear a brass band playing.

"I go out for one day," he moaned, "and I come back to find a disturbance of the peace! Someone will be arrested for this!"

But as he turned the corner, Mr Plod opened his mouth wide in astonishment. He rubbed his eyes in amazement. Then he began to roar with laughter.

High across the street was a huge banner which read:

YOU'RE THE BEST POLICEMAN
IN THE WORLD, MR PLOD!

Standing beneath it were all his Toy Town friends.

"But, Big-Ears," said Mr Plod nervously, "I didn't find the thief who stole your bicycle!"

"Oh, but there wasn't one!" laughed his friend. "We all wanted to thank you for making Toy Town such a safe place to live. I pretended that my bicycle had been stolen so that we could surprise you with this party!"

"Wasting police time is a serious offence," said Mr Plod. "But I am prepared to overlook the matter this once!"

Everyone laughed. Even Mr Plod.

THE GOBLINS
AND THE ICE CREAM

It was a hot, lazy afternoon in Toyland. Sly and Gobbo had been asleep all day.

Sly stretched very slowly.

Gobbo yawned very loudly.

And they both rubbed their eyes.

"Come on, Sly," said Gobbo, getting to his feet. "All this sleeping has made me very hungry. Let's go into Toy Town to have an **ICE CREAM.**"

It was a long walk from Goblin Corner into Toy Town. The goblins felt even more hungry when they got there. At the ice cream parlour, they flopped down and ordered two ENORMOUS ice creams.

"Delicious!" slurped Sly.

PARP! PARP!

Noddy's little car stopped
beside the goblins.

"Hello, Noddy," said
Gobbo. "Would you like
to join us for an ice cream?
You must be very hot
driving around Toyland on
a day like this."

"That is very kind of you,
Gobbo," said Noddy. "An ice cream is just what I need."

Noddy got out of his car and sat at the table with the goblins.

When Noddy's ice cream arrived, Sly and Gobbo gobbled down
what was left in their own bowls.

Suddenly, Gobbo pushed over his chair.
Sly leapt right over the table and they
ran from the ice cream parlour knocking
over Mr Wobbly Man on their way.

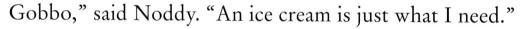

"I say," said Noddy in surprise.
"Where have those wicked goblins gone?
Oh no! Now I'm going to have to pay for all THREE ice creams."

Gobbo and Sly ran and hid behind a market stall. They danced and
cackled with delight. Gobbo suddenly stopped. "All that running and
laughing and dancing has made me very tired," he gasped. "What we
need is a ride home."

PARP! PARP!

"That's Noddy!" said Sly. "Do you think he will give us a lift?"

"Yes, if we ask him nicely," laughed Gobbo.

The goblins leapt out in front of Noddy's car.

"Hello, Noddy," said Gobbo. "We're very tired. You will take us to Goblin Corner, won't you?"

"No I will not, you HORRID goblins," said Noddy crossly. "I had to use the money I was saving for some new tyres to pay for your ice creams. If I don't buy some new ones soon, I won't be able to drive my car. And then I won't have any money at all."

"We forgot our money, that's all," said Gobbo. "If you drive us home to Goblin Corner, we'll pay you for our ice creams and give you two sixpences each for the ride!"

"All right," said Noddy slowly. "But you MUST give me the money. And Sly, you will have to sit on the spare wheel at the back of the car."

So off they set in Noddy's car.

When they had almost reached Goblin Corner, Gobbo pointed to something in the dark wood.

"What's that?" he shouted.

Noddy SCREECHED to a halt and turned to look. Gobbo grabbed hold of a tree branch and somersaulted out of the car. Sly leapfrogged from the spare wheel and they both ran into the woods.

"You wicked goblins!" cried Noddy. "Now my tyres are even more worn and I still have no money. I'm going to fetch Mr Plod."

It was turning dark when Sly and Gobbo heard the PARP! PARP! of Noddy's car in the woods. They scrambled up a tree so they would not be seen.

Then they saw Mr Plod get out of the car and saw the light from his torch shine into the bushes.

"Well, young Noddy," said the policeman. "It's too dark to find those villains now. I wonder if they'll be greedy enough to show their faces in Toy Town tomorrow?"

"Why is that?" asked Noddy.

"It's the ice cream eating competition, that's why," replied Mr Plod. "Let's see what happens tomorrow."

Off they drove back to Toy Town.

The next day it was hot again.

"Just the kind of day for an ice cream eating competition," laughed Sly.

"Yes, indeed!" said Gobbo. "We must make sure Mr Plod doesn't see us."

The goblins couldn't believe what they saw when they got to Toy Town. Huge tables were crammed with enormous, colourful ice creams.

Master Tubby Bear was lining up for the competition with Mr Wobbly Man, Mr Sparks and Clockwork Mouse, and all the other toys were cheering.

"Come on, Sly," said Gobbo. "Let's show them how much ice cream WE can eat!"

"Yes, let's!" laughed Sly.

"Not so fast, you villains!" shouted a voice behind them.
It was Mr Plod.

"Quick!" shrieked Gobbo. "RUN!"

Sly did run... straight into Gobbo.

THUD!

They fell into the bowls of ice cream.

SQUELCH!

And the tables **CRASHED**

to the ground.

Gobbo and Sly were covered in
a sticky, gooey mess!

"I knew you couldn't resist all this ice cream,
you wicked goblins!" said Mr Plod sternly. "Now you must pay
Noddy all the money you owe him. AND you must pay for his
new tyres."

Gobbo and Sly sighed. "We promise!" they said.

"You mark my words," said Mr Plod, pointing at the goblins who
were dripping with ice cream. "Villains like you two will always meet
a sticky end!"

TUBBY BEAR AND THE
DECORATING

Tubby Bear was often naughty. But this morning he was EXTRA naughty.

First, Tubby Bear banged his drum all around the house. It gave poor Mrs Tubby such a headache.

Then Tubby Bear tore up his mother's favourite recipe. He threw all the little pieces into the air to make a snowstorm.

Then, worst of all, Tubby Bear rolled marbles all over the kitchen floor. Mrs Tubby Bear slipped on them and dropped her tea tray.

"I've had ENOUGH for
one morning!" Mrs Tubby Bear
complained to Mr Tubby Bear.
She wiped her hot, furry brow with her apron.

"When you go to decorate Noddy's house, you'll have to take
Master Tubby with you!"

Tubby Bear was delighted that he was going to Noddy's house. "Can
I help you decorate?" he asked excitedly as he walked with his father
along the road. "Can I dip the brushes into the paint? Can I stand on
the ladder? Can I paint the ceiling?"

"No, you may do none of those things!" Mr Tubby Bear told him
firmly. "You would make far too much mess. You are to sit quietly on
a chair in the corner!"

Tubby Bear was very unhappy sitting on the chair at Noddy's house. He frowned as he watched Noddy and his father put up the ladder. He sniffed as he watched them take down the curtains. He wiped away a tear as he watched them open the paint tin. It was Tubby Bear's favourite colour. Bright pink!

"I'm getting a bit bored staring at yellow all day," Noddy explained to Mr Tubby Bear. "So I thought we would paint all the walls a nice pink."

Mr Tubby Bear scratched his head. "But, Noddy," he growled, "you will need more than one tin of paint if you want to paint ALL the walls."

"Will I?" asked Noddy. "In that case, I had better drive my car to the paint shop to buy some more tins. Will you come with me to make sure I buy just the right number?"

Mr Tubby Bear did not know what to do. He thought he should go with Noddy to the paint shop. Noddy could get so mixed up sometimes. But Noddy's car only held two people. That meant leaving young Tubby Bear behind!

"I don't mind," Tubby Bear said from his chair in the corner. He was a lot more cheerful now. "I don't mind being left behind. I promise to stay in my chair!"

Mr Tubby Bear stroked his chin. Could he trust Master Tubby? It was at that moment that Mr Plod the policeman passed the open window. Noddy suddenly had an idea...

"Hello, Mr Plod!" Noddy called. "Are you on your rounds? Could you just peer in next time you pass, to make sure Tubby Bear isn't doing anything he shouldn't?"

"I will indeed," said Mr Plod. Noddy and Mr Tubby Bear felt very happy as they left the house. They were sure Tubby Bear would not do anything naughty NOW.

But as soon as Noddy's car had driven away, Tubby Bear jumped down from his chair. He made straight for the biggest paintbrush and thrust it into the tin of paint.

"I *will* help decorate," he sniggered naughtily. "I will, I will, I will! And one tin of paint is PLENTY for all the walls. As long as I just do spots!"

Tubby Bear started at the wall with the window. He painted great big spots on one side... then on the other side... and then underneath the window.

The naughty bear was really pleased with himself. He thought pink spots looked so smart!

Tubby Bear was just about to paint another wall when he heard whistling outside the window. It was Mr Plod! Tubby Bear hurried back to his chair in the corner.

"Hello, young scamp!" Mr Plod called through the window. He could not see the wall with the pink spots.

"Glad to see you are behaving yourself! I'll tell Mr Tubby Bear and Noddy when I see them."

Tubby Bear smiled as Mr Plod went on his way. The naughty bear ran back to the paint tin but – oh dear! – he ran right into the ladder and knocked it over.

Oh dear! again. As Tubby Bear was jumping out of the way of the ladder, he stepped straight into the paint tin. There was hardly any paint left. Not even enough to paint spots! Tubby Bear returned to his chair very miserable indeed. Very messy, too!

This was exactly how Noddy and Mr Tubby Bear found him when they came back from the paint shop.

"Mr Plod was just telling us how good you have been, Tubby Bear..." Noddy began. Then his eyes nearly popped out of his head. "Look at my wall!" he cried. "How will we remove all those spots?"

"And look at your carpet!" Mr Tubby Bear gasped. "And look at YOU, Tubby Bear. What a terrible mess!"

After a while, though, it was decided that things were not too bad. Mr Tubby Bear said they could easily paint over the spots on the wall. Noddy said he was going to throw out the carpet anyway. It was quite old and would not go with pink walls.

That just left Tubby Bear.

"A hard scrub should sort him out," chuckled Mr Tubby Bear, grabbing hold of one of Tubby Bear's ears.

"Yes!" said Noddy as he grabbed the other ear. "A VERY LONG hard scrub!"

Mr Straw's New Cow

It was a very busy morning on Mr Straw's farm. All the animals had to be fed, the cows had to be milked and the eggs had to be collected. Mrs Straw usually fed the animals, but she wasn't there today. She had gone to look after her sister who was ill.

PARP! PARP! Noddy drove into the farmyard.

"Hello, Noddy my lad, what can I do for you?" asked Mr Straw, rushing out to meet the car.

"Mrs Straw asked me yesterday if I would lend you a hand," explained Noddy. "But I've got **TWO** hands you can borrow if you want!"

"Well, I could do with some help, Noddy my lad," agreed Mr Straw. "Can you feed the hens?"

"Yes, I can," said Noddy.

When Noddy picked up the sack of corn, the hens **CLUCKED** and scratched around his feet. "Here you are, hens! Breakfast!" laughed Noddy, as he scattered the corn on the ground. His bell jingled as he worked.

"That's a funny hen!" cried Noddy. He turned round. A cow was standing behind him, and she was looking at Noddy with enormous eyes. "Shoo!" shouted Noddy.

"It's all right, Noddy. That's my new cow," said Mr Straw who was walking across the farmyard. "She only wants to be friends. Could you collect the eggs now, please?"

Noddy fetched the basket and placed the eggs in it very carefully. He had just picked up the last one, when there was a loud **MOO!** Noddy was so startled that he dropped the egg. Mr Straw's new cow was right behind Noddy, breathing down his neck.

"You naughty cow," grumbled Noddy. "You frightened me. Shoo! GO AWAY!"

"It looks like she's your best friend now, Noddy my lad!" laughed Mr Straw. "I can manage the rest of the feeding, but could you take six eggs to Mrs Tubby Bear for me?"

Mr Straw gave Noddy the eggs and three sixpences for all his help.

"Thank you, Noddy," said Mr Straw. "Don't forget to close the gate as you leave."

Noddy drove out of the farmyard. As he was closing the gate, Mr Straw's new cow began to run towards him.

"Shoo! Go away!" shouted Noddy. He leapt into his car and drove away as fast as he could. Noddy was in such a hurry that he forgot to close the gate. Mr Straw's new cow ran out of the farmyard after her friend.

On the farm it was almost milking time.

"Now, where's that new cow of mine?" Mr Straw asked himself. He looked around the farmyard and saw the open gate.

"I told Noddy to close the gate," grumbled the farmer. "Now my new cow has followed him. Come on, horse. We'll have to find her."

Mr Straw climbed onto his horse and rode out of the farmyard. He made sure that the gate was closed this time, so that all the other animals would be safe.

"I think we'll try Mrs Tubby Bear's house first," Mr Straw said.

"NEIGH!" the horse agreed.

What a sight greeted Mr Straw, as he rode up to Mrs Tubby Bear's house! On her washing line was a pair of Mr Tubby Bear's trousers with their legs badly chewed. A muddy pillowcase lay on the grass and a sheet covered in hoof marks was wrapped around a tree.

"This is your cow's fault, Mr Straw," said Mrs Tubby Bear angrily.

"I am sorry," apologised the farmer. "Is the cow still here?"

"Indeed it is not!" replied Mrs Tubby Bear. "Noddy brought in my eggs, and when he left, the cow followed him."

"And where did Noddy go?" asked Mr Straw anxiously.

"He went to see Tessie Bear," replied Mrs Tubby Bear.

"I must go there at once," shouted Mr Straw, and he galloped off through Toy Town.

As Mr Straw's horse **CLIP-CLOPPED** up to Tessie Bear's house, out rushed Bumpy-Dog. **WOOF! WOOF! WOOF!**

"Bumpy-Dog is very excited," sighed Tessie Bear. "One of your cows frightened him in the garden. Then the cow ate all my flowers."

"I am sorry," said Mr Straw. "Is the cow still here?"

"No," replied Tessie Bear. "I think she was waiting for Noddy,

because when he left, the cow followed him."

"And where was Noddy going?" asked Mr Straw anxiously.

"He went to see Big-Ears," replied Tessie Bear.

"Then I must go there too!" shouted Mr Straw, and he galloped off towards Toadstool House.

Noddy's car was outside Big-Ears' house. So was Mr Straw's new cow. She was trying to eat Noddy's steering wheel.

When Big-Ears and Noddy heard the CLIP-CLOP of Mr Straw's horse, they came rushing outside.

"Go away, cow!" shouted Noddy. "Why are YOU here?"

"She followed you through the open gate," explained Mr Straw. "But I wonder, why is she so fond of you, Noddy?"

Noddy scratched his chin and shook his head. JINGLE.

As soon as the cow heard Noddy's bell, she bounded towards him and tried to pull the hat from Noddy's head.

"It's your BELL she likes!" laughed Mr Straw.

"I will buy her one of her own," said Noddy. "Then she won't need to follow me any more!"

"**MOO!**" said the cow, with pleasure.